Spiro
of the Sponge Fleet

Spiro
of the Sponge Fleet

by Henry Chapin & Peter Throckmorton

Illustrated by Bertil Kumlien

An Atlantic Monthly Press Book
Boston Toronto Little, Brown and Company

ATLANTIC–LITTLE, BROWN BOOKS
ARE PUBLISHED BY
LITTLE, BROWN AND COMPANY
IN ASSOCIATION WITH
THE ATLANTIC MONTHLY PRESS

Published simultaneously in Canada
by Little, Brown & Company (Canada) Limited

PRINTED IN THE UNITED STATES OF AMERICA

Contents

Acknowledgements

We are indebted to Mr. Antony Kalojannis, the mayor of Kalymnos, for his help and advice, and to Mr. Antony Manglis, also of Kalymnos, for his useful suggestions in regard to revision of the manuscript.

Spiro
of the Sponge Fleet

The Fleet Comes Home

THE island of Kalymnos lies at the base of a deep bay facing the mountains of Turkey, which loom up ten miles across the straits. The blue and white houses of the port reach out along both sides of the harbor against the purple and gray hills. A large breakwater keeps the sea winds off the waterfront. Just to the left of the town around a point in a small cove lies the shipyard which services the sponge fleet and the local freight boats.

Spiro Kousaki worked in the shipyard to help support his mother. He was a well-set-up lad for his sixteen years, with broad shoulders and stout legs, stocky and dark like most of the island men. There was an independent, proud direct look about him. This he needed because Kalymnos is a tough, hard-living seaport and the sponge divers are just about the toughest Greeks in all the islands. They have to be to stay alive, with all the odds they have against them.

None of this bothered Spiro; he was born to it. What did bother him on this late November day was the fact that here he was stuck at work tarring the seams of a fat freighter on the very day the last six diving boats of the African sponge fleet were due back in port with his brother Costa aboard. He never yet had missed being dockside when the little ships brought the men back from sea after those long months of danger off the reefs of Tripoli.

Spiro was perched on a scaffold alongside the vessel, a tar bucket in one hand and a stick, wound at one end with wool and dripping with black, in the other. He was jabbing at the caulked seams as if he wished someone and not the ship were in front of him. That particular someone was a crippled old man with a long droopy mustache standing up at the top of the yard keeping an eye on the young yard-rats working on the ships. He watched Spiro awhile and smiled to himself, because he knew well enough what was going on in the boy's head. This old man was called Christos and once had been top *mihanikos* or diver in the sponge fleet. He yelled at Spiro and waved his cane.

The boy thrust his stick into the bucket, leaped off
the scaffold and ran up to the old man, his heart jump-
ing with excitement. He hardly waited for Christos to
say, "The fleet's been sighted. They'll be home in an
hour." He ran to the shed and changed his dirty work
clothes for his clean shirt and pants and was off up the

cliff to the road that leads around the point into the town. He took a quick glance to sea but of course they weren't in sight yet. He ran along by the fishermen's houses on the cliff, past the farmers market, dodged behind the big city hall the Italians had built and found himself part of the gathering crowd that surged toward the central stone pier where the vessels would dock. People grinned at him, for the whole town knew how proud he was of his brother Costa, who was one of the top divers of the fleet. In Kalymnos nothing of greater praise could be said of any man.

When he reached the pier it was already crowded with the families of the ships' crews. He paused to catch his breath, and he heard a yell from a big *deposito* whose stern was moored to the sea wall just to one side. The men on the schooner motioned him aboard, and he sprinted up the narrow gangplank and forward to the mast and climbed up the ratlins where he could get a perfect view of the harbor, over the heads of the growing crowd.

The diving boats that hadn't already been hauled off to the shipyards for repairs all had their flags flying. The pier was swarming with people milling about as relatives of the returning fishermen elbowed their way through to the edge of the pier. Spiro, casting about in vain for a sight of the vessels, looked down on the people. Some of the women were already crying with excitement. Spiro said to himself: Women. Women. Always bawling or

yelling at the wrong time. Everybody knew these boats that had stayed over were the lucky ones, no one dead or crippled.

Suddenly someone gave a shout and looking up Spiro saw the perked-up curving bow of the first of the fleet sliding into view round Point Cali. And then another and another until all six came parading in beyond the breakwater straight for the dock. But which was Costa's? Which was the *Basileos?* They all had lost their paint under the blistering African sun. They were dirty gray, not white and blue and green and orange as they had been when they proudly put to sea seven months ago.

The first vessel headed in to the dock and nosed in alongside the schooner right under him. A bunch of men were standing by the cabin but they all looked alike, bearded and black in their dirty togs. Then he saw one of them pull off his cap and wave it. Yes, that's the way Costa waved. He slid down the shrouds and leaped aboard the sponge boat as she came to rest. Costa saw him and lifting him up in his strong arms gave him a great hug. "Ay, Spiro. What a big guy. How's everything?" and banged him a hard clap on the back.

But Costa was looking over Spiro's head searching the crowded dock for his mother, Dimitra, and his girl, Krysa. Costa turned quickly to Spiro and said, "Brought you something you'll like. It's down on my bunk." He was gone into the dock crowd.

Spiro raced to the dark companionway and stepped carefully down into the black of the hold. He knew the boat, knew Costa had the second best place starboard by the captain's bunk. His eyes got used to the dim light. He saw the bundle and tore it open. He was too excited to notice the acid smell of sponges, stale food and dirty clothes that filled the cabin. Here before him was a fine new diving mask, snorkel, flippers and a long, lean spear gun with a shining blue metallic handle and trigger. Lord, it must have been a good trip for Costa to have spent all this on him. He tried the mask on at once. With this he could see better under water. With the gun he could bring in all kinds of fish for his mother to cook.

He came out of his daydream to notice that the dock was quiet now. The crowd had moved off. Hanging on to his treasures he climbed back into the bright sunlight and headed for home up the hill west of the harbor. He caught up with Costa and the women just as they were going in under the grape arbor to the cool, dim square of the cottage kitchen.

His ma was bustling about bringing out a fresh table-cloth, serving up goat cheese, olives, and dark bread, pouring *retsina* into a clay jug. Costa stood by the sink chopping at his dark beard and getting ready to shave, his clean clothes laid out ready on a nearby chair. Spiro swaggered in and threw his mask and spear on the table. His mother took one look and turned on Costa.

"So that's what you brought him. Diving things. Take them away. I won't have it. Trying to turn my only little boy to the sea. Why can't you men leave an old woman alone with what she's got left?" She suddenly burst into sobs on Krysa's shoulder.

Costa and Spiro looked at each other in panic. Couldn't women ever understand anything? Then Costa strode over and roughly shook his mother by the shoulders. "Stop it, Ma. I won't have this the first minute I get home. Now you listen. Spiro is not a little boy. He's nearly a man grown. Besides this isn't real diving stuff and you know it. I bought it at a tourist shop in Spetsai. Spiro's got to have some fun."

His mother dried her eyes and shrugged. "I can't help it. I hate the sea. How can a woman in this town do anything but hate the sea?"

Krysa led her to the table. "Sit down, Dimitra, and let's drink to the homecoming." The two women looked at each other as if to say: Men! Always acting like big brave kids. Will they never learn?

Spiro got his wine half drowned in water. "*Si-yia,*"

they all clicked glasses and drank. Then Costa filled them again and nodded to Spiro. "*Yasou*, kid, here's to *sfungaria*," and threw his glass on the floor where it crashed. Spiro followed suit and they laughed. The two women looked down their noses. Men!

The world looked good to Spiro next morning when he headed along the waterfront for the shipyard with his gear over his shoulder. A group of his friends had heard of his good luck and followed along, begging for a chance to use his mask and gun or at least borrow his swimming flippers.

"Later on. Later on," Spiro told them full of pride. "I've hardly had a chance to look at them myself."

"Well, anyhow, let's have a look," they begged.

He couldn't resist this and laid the stuff out on the sea wall. The mask was a *Squale* which had come all the way from France. It still was dusted with talcum powder from the shipping box. The new rubber smelled sharp. The fins were even more splendid. They were of Italian make and fitted his feet like a shoe, perfectly tight yet so easy that they couldn't give a man cramps. The gun was the big item, though. It had a pistol grip of blue aluminum and the rubber cords that shot the spear points were very strong when he pulled them back. The sharp spears, three of them, were fastened by cords to the handle. Each spear had double barbs so it would not pull out of the fish. Nothing had been overlooked.

Spiro was proud to have the lads trail him all the way

to the shipyard. But he was careful to hide the equipment in the shed where he dressed, since the others couldn't follow him there. Old Christos examined the gear without a word and then looked sternly at Spiro. "Don't get it into your head, kid, that this junk can make you a diver. You're coming along all right here in the yard. Stick with it and don't get to dreaming. And don't go hanging around those crazy divers."

"No fear," Spiro grunted in disgust. "Costa won't let me near the *tavernas*. But he gave me these to use and I'm going to use 'em." All the morning as he drilled bolt-holes in the heavy decks of a big freighter his mind was exploring the bottom of the coves and bays around Kalymnos. The way the shavings spiraled up reminded him of how the bubbles from the divers' helmets grew larger and larger as they wobbled up and burst on the surface. While he was working he wondered about the grownups. Why were his mother, Christos and the rest always fussing about the sea? "One son at sea is enough," she would say. "You got a nice job son, stick with it, a safe job. I lost your father, and Costa's off with the fleet. You're the only company I have. You belong home." And Christos always telling him how crazy the divers were and to stay away from all that. Why were they always against the sea? Was a Kalymnos boy supposed to grow up a landlubber?

By the time the midday layoff came the *tavernas* along the waterfront were already tuning up to the celebration

of the returning fishermen. The last of the fleet was in
and worries were over for a few months at least. Even
the yard owner couldn't resist the excitement and gave
everybody the afternoon off. This was what Spiro had
been hoping for. He grabbed his gear and hooked a ride
on the old bus that was going around the north shore to
Vathi. He got off a few miles from town and worked his
way down the cliffs to a little secret cove. There might
be big groupers here, so far from town.

Spiro tore off his shirt and pants, slipped the fins
onto his feet, washed the mask, spat on it, washed it
again, slipped the snorkel under the left-side mask strap,
gripped it with his teeth and jumped in. The water
was clear as crystal, like all the island waters of Greece,

and he could see down the rock slope to where the sand began sixty feet below him. He started cruising along the surface under the cliffside. In some places the rock fell straight, in others it sloped steeply to the bottom. Everywhere it was full of ledges, cracks and dark caves. Here groupers lived; the small ones high up the slope, the monster twenty-, thirty- and forty-pounders deep down at the very bottom, at the edge of the sand, where the current brought them smaller fish. As Spiro watched he saw a shadow hanging under a ledge, forty feet below. He took several deep breaths to get oxygen into his lungs and, gripping his spear gun, jackknifed and dove.

Spiro was a good swimmer, perhaps the best for his age in town. Last Epiphany, when the Bishop threw the silver cross into the harbor he had been the one to catch it as it wobbled toward the muddy bottom. And once he had gone out with the naked sponge divers, before his mother had stopped him. They had taught him to handle himself in the water. He was not afraid.

Down he went, his eardrums clicking freely. This was something like. The new mask didn't leak as badly as the

old one he used to borrow from one of the other boys, and the new flippers gave him a sensation of power and control that he had never had before. The grouper hung quietly, suspended in the water, twiddling his fins like helicopter rotors and staring up at him. It looked huge, fifteen pounds at least.

He drew nearer and nearer, then aimed his gun and let fly. The spear clattered uselessly against the rocks. The grouper had disappeared in a cloud of sand. Now Spiro felt the pressure on his ears and his heart was pounding in his chest. Up he went and sat gasping on the shore. Before the afternoon was over and he dragged himself shivering up the rocks to catch the late returning bus from Vathi, he had one rock lobster and two fair-sized mullets. Not so bad. He pretended not to care when the passengers made a fuss over his equipment and catch. Boy, he'd do better than that next time.

He left the lobster at Christos' house when he went through the town. He'd surprise his mother with the two big mullets.

II

The Fleet Gets Set

ALL that winter Spiro had been dividing his time between school and the shipyard but when April came the fleet of little *aktarmades* began to ready itself in earnest for the spring venture to Africa. Suddenly the shipyard came to life and Spiro was working hard there full time. Not that a young apprentice got much pay, maybe a hundred drachmas a week, but there was plenty to learn.

The little yard under the cliff was so full of diving boats pulled up for reconditioning that Spiro could cross the whole yard leaping from deck to deck. There must have been more than twenty boats propped up on the

ways with men and boys swarming all over them. When
Spiro came to work in the morning he could hear the
soft music of the caulking hammers working the cotton
cord into the seams with blunt chisels, and the yells of
the shipwrights and captains sending the yard boys for
paint, tar, lumber and all the hundred small things a
vessel needs to become completely shipshape and sea-
going. He loved it. It was the next best thing to being a
member of a crew. And this he was determined one day
he would be, along with Costa.

When they first hauled the *Basileos* they burned her
fouled planks free of African weed right down to the bare
wood and inspected every inch of her bottom for signs of
the sea worm or *teredo* which can eat into the toughest
Samos pine planking. Then came repairs to the sleek
hull and coats of tar over the caulking. The bright colors
of the upper works were set off with triangles of different
colors fanning down from the scuppers, and a bright
band of color along the strakes from stem to stern. All
the old rigging was renewed and the masts scraped and
varnished. A horseshoe was stuck on top of the *Basileos's*
mast for good luck.

And then came the inside work. All the gathered filth
of the African months was cleaned out fore and aft and
the inner work painted a nice clean white with green
trimmings. The engineers came aboard and dismantled
and cleaned the big single-cylinder diesel engine and
went over the air compressor with great care, for it was

this compressor that fed the life-giving air to the divers far below at the other end of the long rubber hoses. The hoses themselves were inspected and tight canvas coverings sewn on to protect them from chafing on the sharp ledges.

In the town here and there you could see the ship captains and the tenders, who handled the *kolaouzos* or lifelines, carefully weaving small strong cords into a tight line no bigger than Spiro's little finger. These strong lines had to be perfect for they were the only way a diver far beneath the sea could signal to the ship or get signals back from his tender. The divers were going over their new rubber suits, which had to be replaced each year, and fixing the holes in front where the breastplates would be fastened. Rubber cuffs were fitted on the sleeves to close tight around the wrists to keep them water-tight when working.

And then came the great day when the *Basileos* was given her bottom coat of copper paint against the sea worms. She was now ready to slide down the sloping concrete ramp into the harbor and chug across to her mooring alongside the western quay below Spiro's house, where she would take on the equipment and supplies for her seven months' voyage to the faraway African reefs. All this had to be done before Easter when the Archbishop came to town for the final blessing of the fleet.

All winter Spiro's mother had been working part time clipping sponges at the big Apostolis warehouse. She didn't like to live entirely off what money Costa could spare for she wanted him to put it away so he could marry Krysa. She was getting old and wanted another woman around the house and grandchildren to keep the family name alive. Now that the *Basileos* was off the ways the work at the yard was getting slack. So she had begged a morning off for Spiro and told him to come along with her to the sponge dock to meet Apostolis, the owner. He was interested in Spiro because he and Spiro's father had been old friends.

Spiro went along with his mother torn between a desire to stay with the vessel and Costa and a curiosity to see something different. Not just the sponges; he was familiar with them and had been for years. He knew all the different kinds, but he had never been invited into the factory office where there was a sort of museum of sponges and sea oddities collected during the past hundred years from the deep waters of the whole world. Not many boys could brag of this chance.

When they came out of the bright sun into the big dim warehouse Spiro could see the women and some few boys working at the various bins sorting over small mountains of sponges to make sure no faulty ones were packed for export to far away lands. Every one had to be

perfectly clean of any sand or grit and of just the right size.

Spiro was a little surprised to find Apostolis, in a good London suit, sitting with the cutters, a long sharp knife in his hands, handling and judging the most expensive sponges. He was swiftly cutting them into many smaller pieces so as not to waste an inch of the valuable material. It looked easy but he knew it took many years of practice and a smart man to do this without making mistakes.

"Well," said the boss to Spiro, "I've been watching you this past year. I hear good things of you from Christos. Come along, now, I'll take you over and open up the exhibition cases and show you something." Across the street on the waterfront they climbed the stairs of the fine cut-stone offices and went into a large paneled room. Here were portraits of the Apostolis family and a marble bust of a severe big-mustached head of the clan who had founded the company many years before even Spiro's father had been born. On the wall hung government citations for special merit from Turkey, England, Egypt, France and other parts of the world where the company did business.

Strange sea creatures and beautiful shells from the reefs of Africa, the Bahamas and even far Australia were tucked away behind glass cases filled with every imaginable shape and size of sponge. Soft rock-isle wool sponges from the Caribbean, the velvet Bahama sponges, forty-fathom *meletos* from Benghazi and big flat elephant-ear sponges three feet across from Egyptian waters. Any one of these big special prizes would cut up and sell for more money than he and his mother together could earn in a week working in the warehouse across the street.

His mother kept nudging him. "Look, Spiro. Look here. See those wonderful silk sponges, and the honeycombs from Syria. Think what they would sell for, son. Think how good you got to be to learn to cut them for market."

And Apostolis smiled at him and said, "This big round one your dad picked up the year before he was killed. It's so big, with that hole in the middle, that when he surfaced with it it looked like a truck tire hanging over his arm. You only see those once in a lifetime. It was too good to cut. A real museum piece."

Then the boss asked them both to sit down. He ordered little cups of sweet Turkish coffee, and he looked

at Spiro and said, "Son, I know you like the sea. You admire Costa. So do we all. You're a good hand at the yard. Now I want you to think about the real business end of this sponge fishing. It's here right in this place. This is where the money lies. The yard depends on the divers and you have seen fewer and fewer boats go out each year, only twenty last year and this year two more laid off."

"That's right, Spiro, listen to Mr. Apostolis. He knows."

Spiro paid no attention to her, as Apostolis went on, "Spiro, I could use a youngster to train him up in this business. I've got no sons. Start slow and learn it all. Then I could work you into selling and buying. You'd go all over the world, the West Indies, Turkey, Egypt, even to our office in London. Your mother tells me you are learning English at the Greek-American Institute. We'd have to teach you French, too. You seem to have a gift for languages. We buy everywhere, not just Kalymnos. We'll be in business when the divers are out of work and the yards are half empty. What do you think, boy?"

Spiro's mother poked him hard. "Don't be tongue-tied. Tell him yes, son. This is something wonderful for you."

Spiro didn't know what to say to Mr. Apostolis. It was a wonderful chance. No other boy in Kalymnos would have anything like it. Costa's face came before his eyes.

He would have to talk it over with Costa. "I've got to see my brother first," he stammered. "Can I tell you tomorrow, sir?"

Apostolis smiled. "Sure, sure. I know how it is. Too much to take in all at once. You come back here tomorrow or when you're ready. I've already talked this over with Mr. Fokas who owns the shipyard. He thinks it's a great idea."

And so they went home for lunch. Spiro was deeply puzzled. This was something that had never entered his head. For the first time he was glad Costa had made him study English. His mother chattered on full of the good news. She was sure no sane person could resist this kind of good fortune.

In the afternoon Spiro went back to work at the yard with his spear gun and tackle. He couldn't leave them out of his sight for long. Fat old Mr. Fokas came over to him: "So you're going up in the world, young man. This shipyard's not good enough. Going to be a big shot merchant someday." He saw Spiro's spear gun and mask. "Time to drop those kids' toys, son. They only lead to trouble. Anyhow, congratulations, my boy," and he gave Spiro a big greasy grin, as if he had arranged the whole thing.

Spiro found himself suddenly blurting out, "I won't drop these things. I'm the best kid diver around here. And I'm not at all sure I'll take that job. My family are divers."

Old Fokas scowled at him and suddenly hauled off
and cuffed him hard on the head. "You talk like a fool
moutsos. Here, give me those," and he grabbed the gun
and waddled off to the office with Spiro's gear. Spiro
was furious but said nothing. He came muttering back
to the shed where he worked and blurted out the whole

story to Christos. But he got no sympathy in that quarter
either. "Sit down and shut up," Christos told him. "Now
you listen to me. I'm not old Fokas or Apostolis or a
farmer or a shepherd. I used to be a diver along with
your old man. I was the best damn diver in the Kalymnos
fleet." Spiro had to listen. He liked the old man and
what he said was always true.

"You don't remember your dad very well. I do. He
was a good deal like Costa only bigger, and wilder. We
worked the *kolaouzos* for each other and if he didn't get
the most sponges, I did. Well, I had my legs then. I
remember that last dive, not much different from any
other, but we both were trying to prove we were best
man.

"We were working so deep that we agreed to tend the lifeline for each other. The Captain had the say and let us do it. Somehow the clock went wrong that day and we couldn't judge the time under water. They didn't discover it was losing time till sundown, too late. I dove first. I knew something was wrong when I began to feel queer. I didn't say anything when I came up. I thought it would pass. When your old man came up I had collapsed on the deck. I could feel my legs going. I could see your dad didn't look too good either when he took his helmet off. They sent me down again to decompress and try to save my legs. It was too late, but they saved my life. When they brought me up your dad was dead on the deck. He wouldn't let them pull me up sooner, so he could have taken a turn himself. I've been dragging myself around town on sticks ever since."

"Ma never told me this," said Spiro.

"No, she can't talk about it. But she hates the sea. Now you listen to me, boy. All the sponges in Apostolis's warehouse weren't worth those ten minutes. You stay landside. You got the big chance. Old as I am I'll beat you if I hear another word out of you about diving."

Spiro sat there thinking hard. His ma after him. Fokas after him. Old Christos giving him the word and Apostolis holding this big bribe under his nose. What could he do? Looking up he saw Costa sitting with some men under the grape arbor above the yard where they sold ouzo. He slowly made his way up the path. Costa wasn't dead or crippled. He knew how to be careful. He could teach me, Spiro was telling himself. I'm not a wild one. I know plenty already about how scary it is down there. But that's where I belong, at sea with the divers. How can I manage it?

Costa took one look at his glum face as he arrived at the little café. "What's the matter, boy? People been hard on you? Looks like you lost your last friend." The men all laughed. Costa asked, "Where's your gear?"

Spiro told him what had happened with old Fokas down in the yard. Costa raised his eyebrows and nodded at the men and got up and hitched his pants. "Come with me," was all he said.

Spiro followed his brother down to the yard and they marched straight to the office.

Fokas came out of the door and held out his hand. Costa ignored it. "Spiro's through here and you know why."

"But I was only telling the kid . . ."

"Shut up," said Costa. "Now hand over the stuff you took from my brother. No, not to me, to him." Spiro grabbed his gear as the boss shoved it at him. But Costa wasn't through. "Now listen to me," he said. "Maybe you're a big man in Athens, Fokas. You can buy out most anybody in this town. But we don't belong to the town. We go to sea." He poked a hairy finger into the other man's gut. "Yes, you're rich and you're fat but you don't own our ship and you don't own us, and if you

ever raise your hand against Spiro again I'll come up here and knock your ears off."

With that he nodded to Spiro and the two brothers walked on toward the town and home. Spiro was treading on air. He felt as if he himself had just won a big fight. So he was through with the shipyard. Now what?

They could see their mother was very excited when they reached home and sat down to dinner. She recited to Costa the whole conversation with Apostolis at the sponge factory. Costa just nodded and didn't say a word as Spiro sat watching him for some sign of how he felt about it. Finally Costa said, "That's true, Ma, you've done a big job on old Apostolis and he's a good friend to us for making the kid such a grand offer. Now just give him time to think it over. He has a lot to think about."

"But they want an answer tomorrow."

"Sorry, Ma, let's give him one more day. Besides we need him tomorrow to help on the *Basileos*. We're taking her around to the south side for ballast rock. Our no-good deck boy never showed up today. Okay, kid?"

Spiro grinned for joy. His mother shrugged. "I suppose one day won't matter, seeing you need him."

"And Ma," said Costa, "Spiro just resigned from the shipyard." He winked at Spiro and they broke out laughing.

Spiro's mother seemed happy about it all. Now he was free, she was thinking, to go straight to the factory.

Spiro was happy to have his brother begin to take an interest in him. It would be great to be off even for a day on the *Basileos*.

And as for Costa, he really didn't know what to think. He saw plainly enough what was coming up for his brother.

III

Spiro Earns His Ticket

Towns and villages, like people, awake refreshed from the night. When Spiro came out onto the little terrace of his mother's house at dawn and looked down over the housetops to the quiet harbor it seemed as if he had never really seen Kalymnos before. No people, no bustle, no noise, no dust; all was quiet except for those few little early morning sounds that seemed to float alone between the mountain and the sea; the small sound of sheep's bells from the hillside; the distant crowing of roosters from the valley farms; the thin salty cry of a gull cruising the empty harborside. As he stretched and watched the sun poke up over the Turkish mountains across the strait he could hear Costa set down his coffee

cup in the dark of the kitchen. The heavy steps of the
first fisherman clunked down a stone alley toward the
wharf. It was time to go.

The *Basileos* was ready for the African voyage except
for the stone ballast and the final loading of gear and
supplies. Today they were to motor around to the south
beaches for the right kind of flat ballast stone; just
Costa, himself and Captain Nicholaus. It was none too
soon. Easter would come in a couple of days and the
fleet had to be ready for the blessing by the Bishop. As
the two brothers came out onto the wharf below their
house the town was just coming alive. A flock of lambs
with magenta-colored heads, the rams with garlands of
flowers, went trotting by to the marketplace. Everybody
had to buy a lamb for Easter dinner. Other fishermen
hailed Spiro and Costa as they got to the boats. Captain
Nicholaus was already aboard with several large baskets
to collect the ballast. A sizable skiff was towed astern for
getting the load from shore to the vessel.

A few capfuls of breeze roughed up the harbor en-
trance as they chunked slowly out from the breakwater
and headed around the southeast point. Costa shrugged
and looked at the Captain. This might mean the wind
would rise later and make loading impossible.

In about an hour the *Basileos* drew into a narrow bay
between two points of mountain and they threw out a
stern holding anchor and eased her in as close to the
beach as they dared. She had to have a fair clearance, for

the load of stone would set her down more into the water. The men lost no time in throwing the baskets into the skiff and getting to work while the water was calm. They left Spiro on the boat to help unload and watch that the anchor held.

All that morning the little skiff came laboring back and forth and the three of them heaved on the baskets and carefully distributed the ballast below deck so that no matter how rough it might get in a storm, it would stay put and not shift. Finally the job was done, Spiro took a quick dive into the sea to cool off, and Costa and the Captain headed for the beach to visit a friend who lived in a little farmhouse just beyond the shore, where he kept a few sheep, had a vineyard and grew some

lemons and oranges. Very often a retired diver or sailor would retreat to just such a quiet corner of the island free from the town. Spiro was left some bread and olives and told to watch the boat. He could see the men make their way up to the vine-covered terrace of the farmhouse, and if he had to he could reach them with a yell. But it was no skin off his nose to be left behind. It was just what he wanted for he had brought along his snorkel and mask and was keen to be left alone long enough to dive in the neighborhood of the *Basileos*.

For the first half hour things went smoothly for Spiro. Of course there were no sponges in that shallow water

but he did find a small cave not too far from the vessel and managed to spear an octopus which he smashed a great many times against a flat rock on the shore so it would be tender enough to eat for supper. Then on a certain dive he felt a curtain drawn between himself and the silver-shining surface of the harbor above him and he knew at once that the wind had suddenly begun to blow.

He lost no time in surfacing and scrambling aboard

the *Basileos* which already had begun to toss and pull at her anchor. Spiro threw his mask into a corner and took a quick glance up at the farmhouse. The two men there had already felt the sudden breeze and were running down to the skiff where it pounded against the stoney beach. Spiro could hear them yelling at him, but could not hear what they said. He didn't need to, the anchor was already dragging as the heaving of the vessel edged her in toward the rocks. Thoughts raced through his head; should he try to pull up on the anchor line? No good if it was slipping. He jumped for the engine hatch and tried to start the old one-lung diesel. This was a man's job but he somehow managed, after many strong heaves on the fly-wheel, to hear it catch on and hold to a steady plunking rhythm.

He felt more comfortable with the one-lung diesel going. Once started it would just keep plugging along. He turned and saw the anchor was still dragging, then catching for a moment and then dragging again. In a couple of minutes it might be too late. If he let the line go he didn't have room enough to maneuver the vessel by himself between where they rode and the breakers. He had to take a chance and throw her into reverse. All he needed for this job was three hands, one for the tiller, one for the reverse gears and one to pull in the slack of the anchor line as they backed up over it. Well, it was this or nothing.

He could hear the men in the skiff yelling at him as

they drew near. He threw the gears into reverse, cramped
the big tiller under one arm and heaved on the anchor
line. But the little vessel took hold too fast and a coil
of line suddenly caught on the propeller and wound up
to a tight stall before he could do anything. Just then
Costa and the Captain climbed aboard and came running aft to lend a hand. They tried to yank the line free
and turned off the engine. Nothing came loose. Without a word Spiro grabbed the ship's knife from its place
on the mast and dived in under the stern.

This was a touchy job with the keel heaving up and
down in the combers but he managed to hang onto the
rudder post and hack away the line from the propeller.
He quickly surfaced again and yelled to start her up.
"Go, Go," he cried to Costa, "I'll swim out to you." The
men bent to the tiller as the engine picked up and they
just managed to roll and spin along the surf line, almost

broaching, until a relatively calm spell let them turn her nose to sea and ride her out of danger. Spiro, meanwhile, managed to tie the knife to the belt of his trunks and started bucking through the combers after the *Basileos*.

The real danger was over, since he was away from the sharp-bladed propeller. He knew how to cut under the green wall of the piling waves and make yardage before the next one forced him under water.

The men hauled him up over the side and nodded their approval. Everything was now in hand. It would be a wet trip into the squall out around the headland of the narrow bay but this was what these small *caiques* were built to handle with their high sheer and flaring bows. "We'll pick up the anchor tomorrow," Captain Nicholaus said, but the way he looked at Spiro made him feel good. No one blamed him.

Spiro sat under the windward gunwale to keep free of the flying spray and listened to the two men as they began to go over plans for the African voyage which would begin in two days. He couldn't help feeling jealous of the crew as Captain Nicholaus named them over one by one, often using their nicknames.

Kalymnos men sometimes are better known by a nickname they have picked up by chance than by their real name. Nikos he knew as Dimitrios, the first mate and the *kolaouzeros* or man trusted to handle the safety line for the divers and give and send the signals which might mean life or death to those on the bottom. Then came

the seven divers; Panos, who ranked next after Costa;
Limpey, who had been caught by a slight touch of the
bends — his real name was Michaelis — and Niko Blue-
beard; Petro; Wild John; Takis and *Retsina* Chris,
whose weakness on shore was wine. Besides the divers
there were two sailors, and last and least a deck boy for
any and all jobs the others didn't handle. That made a
good load for this little thirty-six-foot *aktarma*, a kind of
trechandiri with high bows and very maneuverable for
quick turns to keep just above the moving divers.

But as Spiro listened the men stopped talking about
the crew. They were talking now in low tones so he
couldn't hear, and then Captain Nicholaus turned to
Spiro and said, "How about you signing on in place of
that no-good boy we had last trip? I liked the way you
handled yourself today."

Spiro was too surprised to say a word. Costa burst out laughing. "It's not a joke, boy, speak up."

"Me? Yes, Captain, yes." Spiro almost shouted and then turned with a frown towards his brother.

Costa knew what was on his mind. "We'll fix it up with the mother," he said.

"How you going to do that?" the Captain asked. "She's got a pretty strong mind, that woman."

"You're going to help me," said Costa. "Now let's plan it out a little before we get home."

"What she going to kick about most?" Captain Nicholaus asked Costa.

"Well, she's going to say he's too young. She needs him home, she's getting old. All that stuff." Costa answered with a shrug. "How about it?" he turned to Spiro.

"Sure, but that's not it really. She'd let me go with Apostolis anywhere. Maybe it's money a little, maybe she wants everything safe now and on land," Spiro told them.

"H'm, money," said the Captain. "Costa, you think that boy's worth much money to me, an apprentice boy like him?"

"I didn't say it to get money," Spiro broke in anxiously. "I'll go for nothing. Only Apostolis offered me some wages in the sponge factory. That's all."

"We give you a deck-boy cut, don't make a mistake. Maybe with luck it turns out okay, too," the Captain grinned at him. "I'll tell you what, boy. I'll come talk to

Mama. I'll tell her we take good care of you. Keep you up top and dry and away from the girls, if we make port, and no *ouzo*. We watch our kids good."

They slid into harbor and tied the *Basileos* up to the pier where they would load on her gear and deck cargo the next day. Then they made for the house, each one going over in his head the arguments they were to use on Spiro's mother.

When they came into the kitchen she was just getting supper. "Sit down, Captain," she said. "Nice to take my boy along today. He's going to be tied up in the sponge warehouse all summer. You heard how Apostolis is giving him the big chance?"

The Captain looked at Costa and Costa took a big breath and started right in. "Ma, we got another big chance for Spiro. Our boat's got to have a deck boy and we want the kid. Just for one voyage."

"No," snapped Spiro's mother. "No, you leave him out of it. He don't need any more chances, not like that."

"I'll take personal charge of him," said Nicholaus. "I'll teach him all about sponges and the African reefs. He won't go under water. Stay right on that boat with me and learn so much old Apostolis will double his wages he'll be so glad."

His mother only grunted as she tended to the stove, so Spiro broke in on his own. "They're going to cut me in for a small share, Ma. I can learn a lot so I'll be twice as good when I come home and go to work for Apostolis.

It's only six months, Ma. Besides I'm going on sixteen. I'm a man. I've got some rights."

"Take it easy," Costa told him and then turned to their mother. "I'll take good care of him. Anybody going into the warehouse needs one trip." He went over and put his arm around his mother.

The Captain stood up and Spiro said, "Only six months, Ma. You owe me this if I'm going to leave the sea for the factory. My dad would have said okay."

The mother turned on the three of them. "All right, go, go. And now all of you shut up talking so much and sit and eat. You give me a headache with all this talk."

Saturday before Easter Sunday was the last day left before the fleet had to sail. The small port of Kalymnos began to take order in the midst of a great hustling about. The painted *aktarmades* were all laid up alongside docks or backed into the harbor wharfs with gangplanks ashore over the stern. Oil barrels, rope, food boxes with pickled peppers, olives, goat cheese, salt beef and the kind of heavy hardtack called *galetas* were carried aboard. The galley was cleaned and set up on the starboard side just aft by the cabin, and firewood was stacked beside it and the diving hose carefully coiled between the cabin and the starboard gunwales. There wouldn't be much room left once everything was in place but it was all done according to an exact plan that many years on the reefs had proved to be the most handy.

Spiro didn't see much of his older brother that day for

the divers didn't have to do the dirty work of loading supplies. They were busy supervising the make-ready of the diving equipment and the hose-lines that would mean life or death to them once they got to sea. The women of the crew brought down lunches to the men as they worked and hung around as much as they dared. The excitement they felt was deep and sad with none of the thrill of coming adventure and gain that gripped the men. The men already had their minds out and away from port, far to sea.

Saturday night was church first then, after midnight, the great release of the end of Lent with dancing in the *tavernas*, parties in the various homes of the fleet's crews and quieter farewells between husbands and wives who would be parted after tomorrow for six or seven months.

Easter Sunday started with a gathering of the village people along the waterfront, everyone dressed in his best. While the people waited for the Marines to come in from the naval vessel in the harbor and act as escort for the Bishop and the holy image of Saint Nicholas, small groups of *bouzouki* and *tsambouna* players came down to the dock and collected crowds around them. Then came the special dance called the Kalymnotikos, a slow movement to a sad music, danced by the young women of the island, dressed in blue skirts and red and white blouses. The crowd made a great silent circle by the wharf.

Now it was time for the blessing of the fleet. First came a navy band from Athens, then the Bishop of the

Islands accompanied by priests in purple and golden robes. They marched between a Marine Guard with drawn bayonets down the long length of the town pier where fifty or more boats fought for position. They came in from their moorings with the tempestuous anarchy of Greece, their diesel engines puffing black smoke, and all at one time tried to nose into the center of the show.

The Bishop aspersed with holy water everything within reach; ships, sailors and the families that crowded around. Three small boys went before the church party holding up crosses on long poles for all to see, and the Bishop's attendants carried the holy Ikon of St. Nicholas, the patron of all sailors.

At long last, with everything sanctified, the Bishop and the important Athenian guests all climbed aboard the *Evangelistria*, the biggest of the *caiques*, and put out into the harbor. This vessel would review the fleet

as it passed in procession. So many climbed aboard that
the little *caique* tilted way on her side and only a miracle
prevented her capsizing then and there.

All the boats loosed their moorings at once and
chugged pell-mell out into the overcrowded harbor. The
crazy diver Dori, standing at the cross-trees of one of the
aktarmades, yelled out, "Hiya, *arrivederci Roma*. Africa
here we come. Farewell to the cheese-eaters."

Spiro was so excited by all this that he began to climb
up the shrouds of the *Basileos* when a sharp call from
Costa brought him down, "You, *moutsos*, come down out
of that. It's reserved for men." This was the first lesson
that showed him where he rated on the vessel — low
man.

Now the harbor was full of circling boats. Many of
them would follow to the African shores but not that
day. Suddenly a cheer broke out from the harborside
crowd as the first perky, brightly hued *caique* chugged
out toward the harbor mouth under the bows of the
reviewing vessel. It was a proud sight to see ship after
ship line up and point out and away for the long summer
adventure. Spiro was leaning over the gunwales of the

Basileos lost to the world. He saw his mother grow smaller in the dockcrowd as she kept waving a little white handkerchief at the boat. Costa was braced in the ratlines in the position of honor reserved for the first diver and Captain Nicholaus stood to the tiller, his eyes dead ahead.

Slowly the town dropped out of sight behind the breakwater, the *Basileos* rounded Cali Point and headed with a steady plunka-plunka-plunka of its big one-lung diesel down the Aegean to the southward.

IV

Off to Africa

As the little fleet dropped Kalymnos and headed around the southern point into the Kos channel the *Basileos* was one of a group of four other boats, the *Electra, St. Georgeos, Tasos* and *Evangelistria*, who all were attached to the bigger *deposito* schooner that went along as a mother boat and floating warehouse. Sometimes the tired crews from the small diving *aktarmades* would sleep aboard the bigger vessel and eat there but on the first day out it was customary to keep on the move and clear the Turkish coastal waters and the Dodecanese islands. The course was now almost due west toward Amorgos in the central Aegean. Fortunately the brisk northerly winds were just perfect for an all-night run across these sometimes very rough waters. The small sails were set now. They were not used much to maneuver with when working the boat but came in handy as an auxiliary for a long reach or running before the northers on the way to Africa.

Not that there was any great hurry about the voyage. After all, they would be gone for half a year, but the first days were useful to break the crew in together if there were new men aboard, and go over all the tackle and supplies and make sure everything was shipshape and properly stored. As the sun went down across the purple waters of the Aegean the men of the *Basileos* could just about pick up the small black peaks of Amorgos on the far horizon and presently the flash of a lighthouse.

Tonight the crew would eat well, as indeed they would for most of the voyage down the Aegean until the diving grounds were reached. The women had picked fresh mountain greens and brought such good home provender as sheep's yoghurt and spring lamb aboard. These fresh things had to be eaten up and the wine drunk, for once the vessels started to work there was only a cup of coffee for breakfast, no lunch and one solid meal at night. No one dared to go down under the sea except with an empty stomach. So the word was eat hearty and fatten up while the going was good. Many long lean days were ahead.

The half barrel of sheet metal which served as a stove was just to the right of the engine hatch, way aft. The cook burned the faggots first while they were still land dry. The kerosene stove would come in handy later. It was wonderful to Spiro to feel the little craft rise and skid across the slightly phosphorescent seas, to watch the masthead sweep across the starry sky, smell the grilled meat, hear a wine cork pop and pick up the stray words of the older men. Their minds and interests dropped all thought of home and took up the usual shop-talk of the sponge fleet.

Spiro braced himself against the butt of the mast and spread *skordalia*, made of garlic and mashed potatoes, on the fresh bread from home and wolfed down the small tender lamb chops that came hot and dripping from the stove. The men gave him his share of wine without question of age and this made him feel warm and good all through. The *retsina* wine of the fleet was light and wholesome, and however intemperate in other things, the Greeks were as a rule moderate drinkers. They even had fresh fruit for dessert. The things that would not keep had to be eaten.

Unless it rained or was stormy Spiro, as low man on board, was expected to find himself someplace on deck to roll up in his blanket. All but the man at the wheel on watch turned in shortly after sundown and supper. The routine of a sponge boat was up at dawn, work all the hours of daylight and hit the bunks around eight-thirty. Spiro found himself a sort of dog's nest among the supplies forward and prepared to sleep, but he was far too excited by the start of this great adventure. The con-

stellations overhead seemed brighter than he had ever
seen them, the motion of the little boat smoother and
more delightful than any he had ever been on. He could
not keep his eyes off the broken flashing of the several
island lights, those they were dropping and those they
were picking up ahead.

The Aegean in fair weather almost always has a visible
landmark for mariners, there are so many islands scattered about. The open central channel between the
Dodecanese and the Cyclades, which they were crossing
this first day out, was perhaps the widest expanse, without a herd of islands in sight, that they would come upon
until next day they reached Antikythera. There they
would turn off to do a little diving on the reefs off Crete.
After that came the two-day run across the Mediter-
ranean to Africa.

Spiro began to go over in his mind this sudden change
in his life. So much had happened in only a couple of
weeks. At home he had been one of the leaders among
the boys. He had had a good job, was a strong swimmer,
the son of a famous *mihanikos* and his brother well
thought of in the fleet. And then came the chance to go
work for Apostolis. That would have really tied things
up and been the solid thing to do. But somehow the
sea had claimed him as it had all his family for genera-
tions. Nothing seemed real at home now as he thought
of it. His mother, Costa's girl, the shipyard, all seemed
like a sort of puppet show. What was real now was the

gabble of waves under the flaring bow of the *Basileos* as it reached before the northern wind, the close stars above the looming dark outline of the islands ahead, the murmur of the men turning in below and the fresh smell of paint, tar and engine oil.

This was real, this was the life he wanted. And yet he could not help but feel a little uneasy about the days ahead. He was low man now, not top boy. Already, ever since leaving port this morning, he was getting little attention from the crew or from Costa. Captain Nicho-

laus, who had been so friendly yesterday, didn't even seem to know he was on board. This might be worse than his initiation into the shipyard. He heaved a sigh and curled up for sleep, resolving to walk carefully in the days to come.

Spiro hardly thought he had been asleep when somebody kicked the soles of his bare feet. It was Costa. "Get up," he said. "First, break up the firewood for the cook. Then swab down the deck. After that report to the mate for cleaning up the bunkroom."

Costa turned and walked aft. So that was it. No chatter, just work. Spiro sloshed his face with salt water from the bucket and began handing out coffee to the crew. Just to the northwest he could now plainly see the dark hills of Amorgos turning bright under the rising sun. The north wind still held good and he could guess they would reach along south of the island and then across the channel to make Ios. But he didn't have much time for daydreaming. It seemed somebody was after him every minute for some job or other. The men well knew what hard work lay ahead of them on the sponge reefs and they enjoyed making the new deck boy hop to it these easy first days at sea.

All that second day they could reach to a brisk north wind. Toward night the small island of Ios drew near. As the wind started to die down Captain Nicholaus took the little vessel in with the others to anchorage in a southern cove of the island. Spiro, to his delight, was now allowed to go overside with his spear gun and managed to pick up a grouper big enough to make a fine fish soup for supper.

That night the five small *aktarmades* anchored about the big schooner that acted as their *deposito*. Before dark the crews gathered aboard the *deposito* to talk over the

future course of their small fleet. The captains got in a huddle and it was decided over plenty of good *retsina* that they'd head for Crete if this fair norther held up, and spend a day or two there trying out their diving gear and maybe picking up some sponge, even if it wasn't of the best African quality.

This trip, he found out as they talked, was a little different from previous trips. Telephone wires had been installed in the air hoses just under the canvas cover, and the *kolaouzeri* and their men had to see just how this was going to work out. This brought up quite an argument among the divers. Some didn't want any newfangled nonsense but the more thoughtful and experienced ones were anxious to try it out. It might save some lives and, God knows, last year the Kalymnos fleet had lost four men and crippled another eight with the bends.

Spiro knew what the bends were. Any Kalymnos boy knew, seeing fine young men come back crippled for life each year, because they had come up from deep dives too quickly. He heard his brother Costa defending the new telephone. "Every year it's harder to get the good sponges. We go deeper and stay down longer and we lose too many good men. If we keep this up every year there will be fewer sponge boats and Kalymnos will get poorer and poorer and have to beg for tourists. Then what kind of men will we breed? Besides, I'm sick of seeing my friends knocked out for life, dragging around town before they're thirty. No sir, and it isn't just the telephone this year. I heard from Athens through the diving school this new scuba tank you take on your back is going to run the old mechanical outfit right off the boards. I tried it once. You are a free swimmer, you can work twice as fast and no lines to tangle."

An old-time diver broke in on him, "You talk like a tourist sport, the kind we get some summers with the fins on their feet taking pictures and acting big." He spat overboard in contempt. "I know what I can handle and I don't change."

Captain Nicholaus said, "We're in business, aren't we? We got to eat. Apostolis who puts money into the fleet, he's got to live good too. Tell us, Costa, how these scubas work."

"Well, you've got your own air with you in this tank on your back. You got a little valve to regulate it. You don't need a suit, so you can't blow up. You don't need a hose so you can't get it caught on a ledge. Your arms and legs are free just like the old-time naked divers. But there's one thing just the same. You come up too fast and you get the bends like anybody else. But they've got the tables for timing worked out very good now. You stick to those tables and take your time, no more bends."

"So we all got to spend half our time sitting around under water?" Costa's opponent broke in, "That's no better than a *skaphandro*, maybe not as good."

Costa didn't answer him but spoke to the Captain: "With this new scuba gear you're going to be able to have three or four men down at once. You'll save plenty of time."

"Anyhow," the old diver answered, "it won't be this year."

"They're going to teach it in the island diving school," said Costa, "and I bet Spiro here will never see the inside of a helmet and air suit if he goes to the school."

So, thought Spiro, grinning to himself in the dark, Costa knows what I intend to do. He resolved as soon as he got back to find out everything he could about this new technique. He had heard it was based on the old Fernez masks that some divers had used but that it went beyond this for efficiency.

And now they got into their skiffs and rowed back to

their small boats for an early morning start. The captains had decided to make a run south of Milos for Rat Island off the western tip of Crete. One of them knew of a good bank there, and maybe they could pick up something worth selling while they got used to handling the telephone lines and checking over the new equipment. Spiro at last felt that the more exciting part of the voyage was at hand.

The open sea was rough but the little double-ended *caiques* were made for just such weather. The high poop and fine stern didn't give the following breakers a real chance to come aboard and the wide flare of the bows wouldn't let the stem dig in running down a particularly steep wave. But they were glad enough to make port. There wasn't much room on board and things were wet. The first day in Crete the *Basileos* left the other boats which were coasting for shallow sponges and made for a certain bank in the channel. The Captain had a long talk with Costa and sent him down after carefully checking landmarks and points to determine their exact position.

The men seemed especially excited and Spiro finally found out why; they were searching for the wreck of a warship sunk in 1942. Spiro and one of the sailors, on the

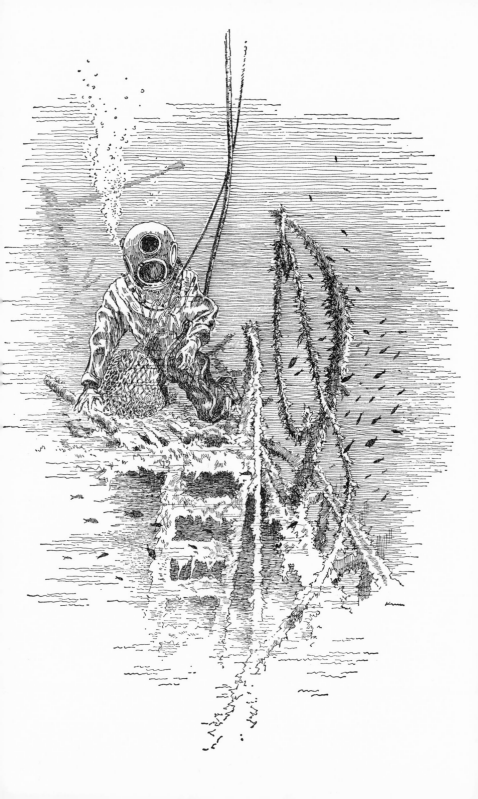

orders of the Captain, got out the heaviest anchor and chain and hung it over the side. The divers went down one by one using the anchor as an underwater platform, while Captain Nicholaus maneuvered the *Basileos* over the spot where he thought the wreck might lie, two hundred feet below. They listened to the directions coming over the telephone. By doing this they did not have to go too deep, and in the clear water they had a good chance of spotting the wreck.

Spiro finally got Costa aside and asked him why they were wasting their time this way. Costa laughed. "Waste time? If you could locate that wreck, you would be right in the middle of a lot of money. I know the man in Athens that owns that wreck: he bought it from the government, but now he can't find it. There are plenty of things in the sea besides sponges."

That night at supper the talk turned to wrecks. Spiro listened, his mouth open with wonder, while the divers talked about their experiences in going down onto a ship that was intact and untouched. Some of these ships were full of valuable junk; lead, bronze and copper. He heard how a man felt when he worked his way into the engine room of a dead ship, and then walked on the white bones of the engineers scattered on the gratings. Some of the old-timers remembered other stranger wrecks. One told of how when he was a cabin boy out of Kalymnos, on a sponger off Turkey they had dynamited a heap of copper ingots, shaped like cowhides. After they had sold all but one for scrap, a man had told them that the things were more than three thousand years old. He then bought the last one to send to a museum somewhere, for more money than they had gotten for the tons of ingots they had sold for scrap.

And this led to talk of what they had heard from even older men about the beginnings of mechanical diving among the Greek sponge fishermen. It was about the first quarter of the nineteenth century when the Greeks from the Dodecanese first began going in any numbers to the African sponge beds. This came in fifty years before the first use of the diving suits and helmets. Before that the diving had been done by men stripped down, holding a stone, making a quick plunge to the reefs and working there while they could hold their breath. There had also been some dragging with weighted nets but the helmet and suit or *skaphandro* technique proved the best.

Captain Nicholaus was speaking: "My father told me that the men were scared of this helmet at first. It was the wife of one of them, on Symi I think, who put it on and went down to shame them. Then they all wanted to do it. But they didn't know how well enough. My God, they lost half their men one year. In Kalymnos the women got together and were going to kill the sponge factor who financed the first diving boat."

There was a silence as the men's minds ran to Symi. Spiro knew what had happened there. Half the population had migrated to Australia to try pearl diving. The place now was dead to the trade although once it had rivaled Kalymnos. Now nothing much was worth the risk except deep diving off Africa. The new plastic sponges had killed the market for the cheap sponges from shallow waters. They were good enough for tourists in Athens but not for serious trading.

A day south from Kythera the first real sponge diving began. Not that they expected much in fine stuff like Turkey Cup or the best Mandruka. That would come later. Right now they had to get the hang of using the telephone instead of depending on tug signals by lifeline. To everybody's relief it worked pretty well and gave both the diver and his *kolaouzeros* on deck a feeling of closer touch. Just how long the telephones would stay in order with constant use on the Benghazi banks no one could guess.

Spiro now hardly knew a moment's rest. He handled the air hose. He ran errands about deck for the Captain who had to stick close to the tiller and maneuver the boat so it stood directly over the divers. When evening came he had to stamp the dark, slimy day's catch of

sponges on the deck to squeeze all the milky white juice out of them. At night he helped hang the day's take overside to wash out.

Long before dawn, and before the first diver slipped into the suit and staggered clumsily to the dressing bench in the bows, Spiro and the sailors had to clean the sponges of the day before. These had changed overnight from black balls to brownish white lumps, full of flecks of black of the sponge colony which had rotted off overside the night before. It was hard work getting out the remnants of the live colony of sponges, so that the skeleton, the thing we know as a sponge, would not rot when packed into the big burlap sacks that were lashed to the port side rigging. They had to dip each sponge into a bucket of water and smash it against the deck many times before it came clean and could be safely stowed.

At night they anchored alongside the *deposito*, and enjoyed the big meal that had been cooked on board. The deck boys always ate last, and were expected to clean up the mess. Often there was only spaghetti or dry rice for them, with the cold and greasy leavings of the stew that had been eaten by the divers. Spiro had been tired before, but never tired like this. If the Captain or Costa or one of the sailors caught him trying to snooze during the day it was "*Moutsos*, get my cigarettes! *Moutsos*, bring me a cup of water! *Moutsos*, clean up that mess! *Moutsos* . . ."

Spiro began to wish he had stayed home in the shipyard and had never seen the *Basileos*. He began to nurse
a deep grudge against Costa, Captain Nicholaus and
the sailors. Especially against one called Antonio, who
never let him rest. Then, one night he crouched in the
shadow of the deckhouse with Janaki, the *moutsos* from
the *Evangelistria*, waiting for the men to finish a suc-
culent stew of salt beef, tomato paste and onions, with a
smell of some delicious herb that made their hungry
bellies squirm. Spiro heard the familiar voice of Captain
Nicholaus say to another of the captains, "You should
get a boy like the one we got, that doesn't mind work.
I'd rather have a boy like that than all the bums from
Piraeus . . ." Spiro suddenly thought better of the
speech he had been composing, the one he was going to
make the day he told Captain Nicholaus to take his ship
and give it to the devil.

That night the captains decided that everything was
working well enough, and while the weather held it was
time at last to make the long run for Benghazi. For three
days and nights under a hot sun the little fleet made
southeast out of sight of land across the open Mediter-
ranean. The big one-lunged diesels plunked steadily
away, giving them a speed of about six knots. The sails
gave them an extra knot or two when the wind held, and
prevented too much rolling in the big seas. On the third
day the wind dropped and the sea fell calm, with only
a long swell from the west. It was very hot on deck, and

the hold was like an oven. Everyone tried to stay in the shade of the awning that Captain Nicholaus ordered stretched over the boom. That evening they saw the low yellow sands of the Cyrenaican coast. The straggling *aktarmades* pulled together around the depot ship, so that they would look like something when they made Benghazi and reported to the authorities there before they began to work the sponge banks. Spiro felt like an old hand as he held onto the stays and craned his neck to get a look at the small yellow and white houses of the Arab seaport. Kalymnos, home, and mother were now far from his mind. He kept feeling his lip, wishing that the first fuzz of his mustache would grow strong and black like Costa's. What with the sweat and the sun, he thought it might.

They began diving next day on the shallow banks off the coast, working in from ten to twenty fathoms. This was to accustom the divers gradually to deep water, for a man that began diving deep after a winter of drinking and eating could be caught by the bends. Spiro soon got used to the monotonous shore, often out of sight in the desert haze. He learned to endure the miserable nights anchored in the open sea, riding to the big swells on a long warp. The good fresh food from home ran out, and now it was rice and beans, or beans and spaghetti every evening, washed down with stinking water from the oil drums on the depot ship, with an occasional hunk of salt beef or dried octopus roasted in the coals of the wood

cooking fire. In the middle of the day everything was dead on board. The men crawled into what patches of shade they could find, while Spiro watched the depth gauge on the cabin front and every five minutes called the depths of the diver below. Nikos, the *kolaouzeros*, crouched in the very bows of the ship like an old, wizened figurehead, his ancient straw hat hanging around his ears and nothing alive about him but his alert black eyes and his sensitive fingers, which followed every movement of the diver. Spiro became friends with old Nikos then, because they felt that only they, along with the hose man and whoever was at the tiller, were responsible for the divers. Nikos never said anything, but Spiro knew he liked the way he had learned to call the depths, and it pleased the old man when Spiro noticed that he was out of cigarettes and brought him some from the cabin.

Spiro learned a lot from old Nikos: how to make the

intricate lashings that held the diver's iron- and lead-shod boots to his feet, and the even more intricate knots that lashed the diving weights to the diver's breast. He was very proud the day that old Nikos let him lash Costa's diving weights, and he tied the knots with special care, knowing that Costa's life depended on him. Spiro now realized why a captain was so fussy about his crew, and why when one man of a crew was in trouble ashore, the others always rallied to help, without question, for the divers on an *aktarma* were life and death comrades.

The boy would never forget the time that Nikos let him hold the *kolaouzos* when Captain Nicholaus was asleep one day and the telephone had to be adjusted. He now knew how it felt to hold the life of a diver in his hands. It made the hardship of being hungry all the time a little easier to bear.

They did well off Benghazi until the weather got worse. Spiro was as happy as a ship's boy can be, on a sponge boat off the coast of Africa in the summertime.

Then one day Captain Nicholaus and Captain Michaelis, of the *Evangelistria*, decided to cut loose from the fleet and head down the coast to the reefs off Tunisia. The two little ships loaded up with fuel and provisions from the depot ship, and pointed west down the coast, taking a week to run the four hundred and fifty miles to the new grounds. They would stop for a half day when the weather got good, and then run on when the wind made up and diving was difficult. Off Tripoli they hailed another Kalymnos boat, the *Katina*. Her captain was an old friend of Nicholaus's and he advised that they go on toward Kerkennah and the rich shallow banks of Tunisia at once. The captains argued over this nearly all night, their little ships rolling in the swells. The crews anxiously waited and listened, crouching in the shadow, away from the space on the fo'c'sl head where the captains sat in the glare of a pressure lamp, and drank and talked and smoked and cursed the weather. In the end they decided to give up Kerkennah and head for the Austria reef, just south of Pantelleria and Sicily. Here there were plenty of sponges and shelter from the unseasonable weather.

V

Spiro Proves Himself

The diving was serious business indeed, not so much because of the depth of the water but the hazard of the rock formations that made up this small underwater plateau less than an acre in extent. It was natural sponge ground, a real honeycomb of dark elongated caverns. Long fingers of rock reached up from several hundred feet down to within ten fathoms or sixty feet of the surface.

The Captain explained the reef to the new divers who hadn't yet tried it on previous voyages. He told them where the fine silk sponges and the *mandruka* honeycombs grew under the sharp ledges and warned them, as they worked the sides of the plateau in and out of the caverns, against getting the lifeline or the air hose hung up and caught on the sharp projections of rock. This was a place for expert and experienced divers but every man on the *Basileos* was full of confidence and eager for his turn to search for the valuable plunder of Austria Reef.

The little ship rocked softly in a slight swell, and there was scarcely a breath of air when the first diver had his helmet tightly screwed on and slid overside from his seat forward by the ladder on the starboard bow. The hose was paid out slowly, the pressure gauges for the air kept steady, and presently the bubbles came up evenly from a fixed position close to the boat as the diver moved gradually along the face of the hidden cavernous plateau. The diver must have been about one hundred feet down and his thin voice could be heard plainly from the hissing loudspeaker on the cabin bulkhead. There was great quiet aboard the boat and more than the usual tension when they had a man down. This particular reef was so dangerous to work that the slightest slack in the hose might give it a chance to catch on a sharp edge of rock. If this happened and the diver was trapped for too long a time on the bottom before his hose could be freed, then almost certainly he would get the bends as he came up. So men watched the clock, the lifeline for signals, and the action of the hose with great care.

The first man down when his time was up surfaced with a handsome catch of slimy green-black sponges, a real money catch, and everybody on the *Basileos* felt relieved and glad. He told them it wasn't too bad. The next man down worked a new face of the reef and the boat maneuvered gently along to keep over him. The sun was well up now and the earlier tension aboard the boat relaxed. Perhaps too much so, for the crew was pretty tired by now. They had picked up almost a hundred pounds of good quality sponge a day and wanted to keep going before rival boats began to work this new ground.

It was hard to tell when they first sensed trouble. Perhaps Nikos had become a little overconfident as he held the lifeline and missed some faint signal. Maybe Takis, who was the *mihanikos* now on the bottom, because he was young and ambitious had not taken enough care in handling his hose among the reefs. It was just about noon when the old alarm clock showed it was time for Takis to come up. Nikos gave the lifeline three tugs, which was his signal, but nothing happened. He tried the telephone and got no answer, just a faint buzzing. He jerked again, and by his expression both Costa at the compressor and the Captain at the tiller knew something was not right. Nikos shrugged and shook his grizzled head. He looked worried. His old fingers could read every sign on the lifeline from long practice, and it now felt to him as if something were caught tight. The hose didn't look right either, although Takis was still breathing well, as the even flow of bubbles indicated. He prob-

ably didn't know anything was wrong between himself and the boat. He'd find out soon enough when he began to move along the reef again, but he probably felt it was about time to come up and was working on one place as he waited.

Nikos waved quickly to the Captain at the tiller who immediately knew what was wanted. He threw the engine into gear and eased the *Basileos* directly over the stream of rising and expanding bubbles in order to create a little more slack on the hose. Nikos jerked the lifeline again and felt rock. Costa came over and took the hose away from a sailor and very gently began taking it in.

After a few feet it too held fast where it was tangled far below on some jagged pinnacle of reef. To pull on it now might sever the air line and that meant a dead diver.

The Captain slowly began to turn the boat in a circle, hoping to free the hose gently. Nothing gave. He over-ran the column of bubbles. Nikos yelled at the Captain, and Costa slacked off extra feet of hose from the boat. Everything then came to a dead stop and the boat drifted back a little with the current. Everybody watched the bubbles coming up and swelling at the surface before they mildly exploded into the air. So far at the very bottom things were normal. But everyone knew they faced a crisis and every mind was turning over some desperate remedy. The men in the boat could not dive to help him, for the compressor was rigged for only one diver.

Spiro dropped his work forward where the next diver was being dressed and slid back beside the stove where his mask and flippers were tucked away under the firewood. Instinctively he got them out, watching Costa and the Captain. The men both were so intently feeling at the signal line and trying to free the hose that they didn't notice as Spiro slipped into the water and swam over the column of bubbles coming up through the clear water from over a hundred feet below. He took a shallow dive and looking down he could see the top of one of the rocky pinnacles where the bubbles worked their way out of a dark cleft in the rocks. The hose line rose straight and stiff from this cavern. That was where it was caught.

When Spiro surfaced, the men on board had noticed what he was up to and were now yelling at him to come over to the side of the boat. Costa called at him, "How deep can you see?" The Captain left the tiller for a moment and came to the gunwale.

"The hose goes down about sixty feet," said Spiro. "I can see it clear. Then it goes under a ledge. Takis is far below that."

"Which way is it caught?" Costa asked as the Captain made for the tiller and got ready to slip the gear into action. The first thing to do was to slack the hose. Spiro swam over to the place directly above the diver and the Captain eased the *Basileos* up to where he was treading water. Costa gave a pull and about ten feet of lifeline came free. Now both the lifeline and the hose were straight up and down. Nothing more gave. It was dangerous to pull too hard on the air hose. The Captain looked at Costa and then quickly signaled to Spiro to go down and take another look.

Spiro was excited but not scared. He took several deep breaths and, buckling over, kicked himself down along the lifeline toward the gray shadows of the reef. His ears cleared easily. Catching fish every day had got them accustomed to pressure and they opened up without trouble. About twenty feet down he hung onto the lifeline for a few seconds. His heart was pounding but the

pressure here didn't bother him. He made out where
the hose was caught far below over a sharp out-cropping
of rock that might cut it in two if the diver, who yet
didn't realize he was hung up, tried to move around or
free himself. He saw a long black patch of hose where
the canvas had already been torn off. This was what had
wrecked the telephone line as well. His time was up. He
had to turn and make for the surface. By this time he was a
good fifty feet down and the sea above looked like a big
dish of quicksilver. His fins pushed him up in short order
and he grabbed onto the ladder of the vessel and caught
his breath. All the way up he had been letting it out of
his lungs gradually.

The Captain and Costa both were calling overside at
him. "What did you see? How bad is he caught? Is the
hose cut any?"

Finally the Captain began giving orders to the sailors

and came over to the ladder where Spiro was now resting. "How deep were you?" he demanded.

"About ten fathoms," said Spiro.

"Can you make it deeper?" he asked the boy.

Spiro nodded. He knew he could make it some deeper but there was always the waste of time getting down. A sailor came over with about twenty pounds of ballast rock in a bag. The Captain grabbed it and handed it to Spiro. "Let this take you down, then drop it. We'll get you a knife. Try and cut the lifeline loose. We'll tie another to your wrist. Don't move on the way down. Don't waste your breath, you've only got three minutes at most. If you don't make it this time we got plenty rocks."

Costa leaned over and slapped his back with a grin and handed him a sheath knife with a cord on the handle. "Tie it to your wrist."

"And don't cut that air hose," yelled the Captain. "If you do, don't bother to come up again." He leaned over the side and held the sack so the stones were in the water. "Tell me when you're ready," he said, "then grab this weight and get down there right along the line. Cut the line and try to free the hose. Give me three jerks on your own line and we'll help you up. Got it?"

Spiro got it. This was the old way, the old style of diving that the Kalymniots had carried on in the days before the helmets and Fernez gear. In those great days, Spiro knew that the naked divers had gone one hundred and eighty feet holding onto a flat stone. He now sent up

a little prayer of thanks for all the days with the mask back home. He gulped in deep drafts of air. If the great divers could make it to thirty fathoms he could do twenty. Then he looked at his brother and nodded to the Captain.

He grabbed hold of the sack of stones and flipped over. Down he went like a streak. Nothing like this had ever happened to him before. At twenty feet his ears hurt and he convulsively grabbed fast hold of the diver's lifeline. He came to a stop and the bubbles in his ears cleared with a pop. The ledge was still well below him. He slid on down and down, passed the tip of the rock where the weed began and came into a cave where little schools of red rockfish scattered before him. He came to the ledge where the hose was caught and let go the sack of rock to be free to hang onto the lifeline and at the same time use his free hand on the hose. He worked automatically with just one word racing through his head, faster, faster, faster.

He managed to get a section of the hose between his legs and pull it loose from the nearest ledge but something still held it. Just below him the hose was pinched between the rock and an old rusted anchor-fluke. He pulled himself into the narrow bottom of the crevice. His heart began to pound. Maybe he hadn't been under so long, but the work was what made it bad.

Meanwhile, up above they kept maneuvering the boat around and he had now a little slack on the hose to work with. He tugged and, just as he thought he couldn't make another move, it slipped free and he caught a quick glance of the diver far below him looking up and sending a sudden signal of recognition about what had been done.

Suddenly he remembered to slash the caught lifeline and then blindly grab hold of his own and give it a yank. He almost blacked out as he felt the welcome heave on the line tied to his wrist. He tried to help by kicking his way up and gradually letting out the breath that seemed to burst his lungs. He was so far gone by the time he reached the surface that he knew nothing until he came to on deck with a great gulp of brandy burning his throat and Costa and the Captain leaning over him. He gave such a splutter of salt water and liquor they both began to grin. He lay still heaving in beautiful breaths of air but he was enough alert now to hear them say, "You did it, man. He's on the way up." Somebody reached down and pressed another swallow of brandy to his lips. He heard Costa tell the sailor, "Give the man what he needs."

They let the diver Takis come up very slowly. He had overstayed his time on the bottom and, even though he didn't know it yet, had come very near death. There was no use giving him the extra risk of bends. The bubbles that might by now have forced themselves from his lungs into his bloodstream had to have time at the different rest levels to work out. Just like the breath bubbles that escaped from the helmet, the small ones at a hundred feet, once the pressure relaxed, became big ones near the surface. If this happened to bubbles in your bloodstream it would be just like a soda or champagne bottle letting go when the cork was popped. Only when this little explosion happened in your arteries it was death.

The crew didn't make much open talk about Spiro's job on freeing the lines. They all expected to take risks and were ready to. But he could tell from the way they began to treat him that he no longer was going to be kicked around as a green kid. He belonged. He stood as a man among them. Takis, once he had been decompressed and hauled up onto the deck, was the only one who made anything personal of it. When he got the whole story he came over to Spiro and put his arm around his shoulder and said, "Maybe I can do a trick for you one day when you get to go down." Spiro knew he had made a friend for life. Two people who have faced death together are never the same again with each other. There's that little debt they owe to God and each other that stays special.

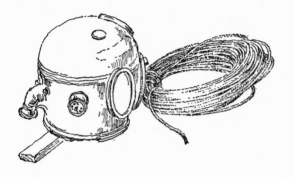

VI

The Forty-Fathom Reefs

AFTER the excitement of Takis's rescue the days fell
into a hard-working routine with little exceptional inci-
dent for Spiro. Even if he was accepted by the men of
Basileos more or less as one of them, his tasks on board
remained the same repetition of dull chores. Cleaning
up, swabbing deck, squeezing the stinking sponges and
the rest. Only on certain occasions was he let in on
helping with the compressor or fixing the engine. Toward the end of the hot summer he was permitted to
help dress the divers in their heavy equipment.

After the Austria Reef the Basileos steered east along
the Benghazi Banks, until they met the *deposito* at last

by the deep forty-fathom grounds where the finest sponges hid in the mud two hundred feet down. Here great care had to be taken and constant alertness with less time per man at such a depth. But the rewards had been good so one day Captain Nicolaus called a halt to rest his crew. He brought the *Basileos* inside a cove where they were out of the wind.

As the crew were sitting around in the afternoon playing cards the Captain turned to Costa and said, "If Spiro thinks he wants to stay at sea next year maybe now's a good time to let him try on the suit. It's calm here and only twenty or thirty foot and an easy bottom. He might even pick up a roller or two for himself." Rollers are detached sponges that roll along the flat sands and are easy to find. Costa looked over at Spiro and said, "How about it, kid?" Spiro, all grin, was on his feet in an instant and headed for the rigging where a diver's suit was hung up to dry. The men dropped their cards and came forward. Here was a novelty that might promise a laugh or two, to see a greenhorn try to handle a *mihanikos'* suit for the first time.

Spiro himself didn't have a doubt. He'd helped dress the men and seen them jump over the side and work with slow ease along the underwater reefs as he gazed down with his diving goggles from near the surface. Costa alone seemed a little serious. He remembered they had promised their mother not to let Spiro dive. Well, this wasn't a real dive, just a kind of practice wetting down. He shrugged and grabbed the diving suit from his young brother and told him to sit down at the divers' seat.

Spiro had felt that something like this might happen for a long time and was ready for it. Now that the moment had come he felt a cold excitement grip the pit of his stomach. This was for real. He ran to the place where he slept on deck and got a pair of rubber bands he had fashioned from an old inner tube. These would hold the big wool socks which Costa now handed him from slipping loose on his legs. He sat down on the divers' seat and began to pull the heavy canvas diving suit on over his legs. His feet were a little small for the shoes but he stood up and pushed his wrists through the tight rubber cuffs of the sleeves. They came nearly to his elbows as Costa pulled them up his arm. They were made for full-grown men with thick wrists.

Spiro stood up now and walked a bit to get used to the

feel of the suit. Costa handed Spiro the box that held the
bolts and clips for fastening on his breastplate where the
helmet would be screwed on as the last thing. The breastplate was heavy and cut into his collarbone but he didn't
care, he was going down as a *mihanikos*. His mind was
in a whirl. Costa helped him work the piece over his
head and pull the heavy rubber neck-piece of the suit
over the breastplate bolts. They now fitted the clips over
the bolts and tightened the wingnuts so no water could
force itself in.

One of the other divers knelt at Spiro's feet and adjusted the heavy diving boots with the lead soles and
strapped them tight. This would help him balance and
keep his feet on the bottom. Spiro had been allowed to
do this for the *mihaniki* many times, and it gave him
a great kick to think that one of these men was now
doing it for him. Now the leads were put on and the men
discussed how to rig him. His difference in weight was a
problem. A front lead was lashed low, almost across his
belly, so the weight would help him to keep tipped
slightly forward.

The danger down below was to get tipped backward
and lose control of the hose and air line and so get blown
up and go shooting to the surface. The whole game was
a nice balance between weights and air in the suit so a
man could go tiptoeing gently along the bottom and keep
in balance.

The straps were pulled tight under Spiro's arms and

the lifeline or *kolaouzos* was fastened firmly to his breast-plate. Now when he tried to move Spiro felt like an undersized lobster in an oversized shell. Everything seemed to interfere with everything else. He had a moment of panic. What if nothing worked when he got below? Then he remembered that all this was arranged for underwater where all the weight would be different and he'd have air in his suit. He looked around at the clock and the pressure gauge on the cabin front and saw the eyes of the men on him. He felt unnatural and still scared, but he smiled at Costa. He had heard plenty of stories about what could happen to a man on his first dive. He could break his face plate and maybe drown before they could get him up or, if he blew up and ballooned, he could tear his suit away at the breastplate and maybe drown that way, he could . . .

"Spiro!" Costa saw what must be going through his mind and spoke sharply to him. Costa was dead serious. He didn't anticipate trouble from a shallow dive but he wasn't taking it lightly, either. "Spiro. How many pulls for up?"

"Three."

"How many for everything okay?"

"One."

"And for more slack?"

"Two."

"Good." Costa grinned and handed him the weighted descending line which would steer him straight to the bottom. He could hang onto this and adjust his weight before going all the way down. A sailor picked up Spiro's heavy left foot and hung it over the side. The lead shoes were so heavy Spiro could not lift his leg over the side by himself. When he tried to, all he did was feebly kick the gunwales. He took a deep breath and tried to look impassive and at ease. It was too late to change his mind now. He saw Costa out of the corner of his eye coming up the starboard side of the grating with the diving helmet under his arm. Spiro picked up the *apoche* or sponge netting and tied it to his breastplate. He now heard the tune of the engine change as it picked up the load of the compressor which a man had just thrown into gear.

Spiro was sitting on the seat forward by the starboard bow ready to go overside. Costa came up with the helmet, "Just remember, Spiro, don't lean back, keep a forward tilt, or you may get blown up and balloon." As he said this he eased the helmet over Spiro's ears and engaged the threads where it screwed into the breastplate. The boy heard the lock snap with a click. This was the moment. He squeezed the descending guideline hard and when Costa gave him the rap on his helmet he jumped, turning in a half circle, and splashed clumsily into the sea.

The air from the hose line now roared into the helmet and he could smell the oil from the compressor. He floated, feeling himself getting lighter and lighter as the air came into his suit. Then he hit the valve with his head and sank slowly down under the surface clutching the shot line with his left hand, so as to keep it free from his lifeline and the air hose. He looked out the glass port of his helmet and saw above him the receding black hull of the *Basileos* and the darkening blue-green of the sea all about. He had a desperate moment trying to think all at one time of the numerous instructions Costa and the Captain had given him. He felt the increasing pressure of the sea grip his legs and the pressure on his body, and the incoming air from the hose seemed to clog his ears all at once. He gave a shout to clear his ears and hit the helmet valve again.

Now for a moment he felt more in control of himself as he let the shot line slip through his fingers. After all it was only twenty feet or so to the bottom. He let go of the line when he saw the sandy bottom with its patches of weed rise up to meet his heavy boots. Slowly the two came in contact and he suddenly felt safe. He was standing on the sandy bottom at last. The rocks nearby were covered with big black sponges, not the kind that had any value. The real money sponges would be growing under the ledges in deeper water.

And now the air seemed to roar in his ears, the hose line between his legs seemed to draw him backward and he felt trapped as if he were in a wind tunnel. He remembered old Nikos up there with the *kolaouzos*, gave two hasty jerks on his lifeline and the pressure eased. He took a couple of tentative steps towards the rocky ledge but the hose seemed to drag him sideways like a crab. He raised his right arm to pull the hose freer and some bubbles burst out at his wrist and let water inside his suit. He quickly dropped his arm. He remembered Costa telling him, "Keep your arms down, kid. Keep your elbows in close or you may lose control."

He was almost to the rock now and could see some small fish scattering. He thought for a moment of the big eels that sometimes lived in the caves but dismissed the idea as cowardly. The sight of a fat grouper looking at him steadily a few yards away made everything suddenly seem familiar. But he wasn't fishing now, he was after sponges. His first real good African sponge.

His eyes were now accustomed to the undersea light. He saw a fine sponge, pulled himself carefully over to it and grabbed hold. It came away easily in his fist. He remembered what old Christos had told him back in the ship yard, "Boy, when your dad and I hit that African bank there were sponges all over the place and they seemed to come to hand as if they liked us . . ."

Spiro began to grin and feel confident of himself, and then he suddenly felt strange. He began to float up. He was too light. While getting so excited over his first sponge he had forgotten to hit his air valve. His suit was beginning to swell up all around his body, lighter and lighter. He desperately pushed the valve all the way with his head, but too late, nothing happened. He felt himself falling over backward. He struggled to regain his balance but was flat on his back now. He kicked his feet and was amazed to see them rise in the water away from the sandy bottom. He tried frantically to use his arms but couldn't even bend them any longer. The diving suit was stiff with air and he felt his whole body begin to rise straight up toward the silver surface of the sea.

The air roared in his ears and the light got brighter and brighter. His helmet had sprung up higher than his head, his feet were out of his boots and his arms were spread-eagled stiff as boards. It was too late to do a thing. He had ballooned.

Spiro was scared but didn't have time to do much about anything. Flat on his back he came wobbling up to the glittering surface of the sea unable to use hand or foot. He suddenly came popping up out of the water like a wounded dolphin and bobbed about on the waves. But only for a second. One of the men jumped in and grabbed hold of the big, fat suit and shoved him like a raft over to the diving ladder where others took hold and pulled him

onto the deck. Then another sailor jumped on top of the swollen suit and released the air valve and Spiro heard the sharp hiss of the escaping air and the release of pressure on his ears. There was no danger of bends here because he had not been down far enough or long enough.

They unscrewed his helmet and pulled the suit off. His feet had pulled right out of the oversized boots and one of his sleeves had begun to leak. Spiro suddenly realized that if his suit had sprung a leak from so much air the lead shoes and metal helmet would have sunk him like a stone to the bottom. As he staggered to his feet he could not keep his legs from shaking. This was awful. He was not a coward. He had a hard time not weeping with rage at what had happened to him. What would the men think now?

He soon found out. They stood around laughing and making a big joke of the whole business. One of them held up the sponge Spiro had gotten from under the reef. "Look," he yelled, "a real African silk."

Costa noticed how hard his brother was taking it and came over to him. "Okay, Spiro, take it easy. Almost everybody does this the first or second dive. It's not easy to learn to be a *mihanikos*."

The other men nodded at him. One of them said, "I bet there's more than half of us did just what you did. Now you know. Next time down you'll really begin to handle your suit right."

Spiro took a long breath and turned to Captain Nicholaus, "Please, Captain, let me go down again. This won't happen a second time."

The Captain grinned and looked at Costa. "Fat chance, boy. What if your ma hears about this when we said we wouldn't let you dive?"

Costa looked at Spiro and said, "This wasn't a dive. He just tried on the suit at twenty feet. I'm not going to let him dive." He turned to the crew, "Nobody's going to say he made a dive. He just tried on the suit for size and it didn't fit so good." They all laughed and Spiro felt better. "Now squeeze out the sponge on the deck and hang it over tonight to clean out. You may want to keep it for a souvenir."

So Spiro went back to the routine chores of the vessel for the remaining weeks of the season and it was a good season for the *Basileos*. Only one *mihanikos* got a touch of bends and they managed to get him down and under to decompress before he came to harm. Every day they got up at dawn. Every day Spiro helped with the hose or the compressor or in dressing the divers, and every night he trampled the day's catch of sponges and watched the milky white seed run through the scuppers back into the sea. He found it hard but healthy, getting only one square meal a day and half the time when they didn't get to the *deposito* it was only pickled peppers or beans, with a little salt beef, olives, rice and hard bread. He toughened up and began to look more like the man he felt he was. After all, when they got back he'd be having

his sixteenth birthday in November, and for a Greek island boy that was a man's age.

Then one week the Basileos could operate only half time because of a definite change in the weather. The fall winds had set in along the coast and it was becoming far too risky to dive in troubled seas. Besides, the crews had been going full tilt now for months and there wasn't a man in the fleet that wasn't pretty beat up with fatigue.

One day Captain Nicholaus called the crew together. "I'm going over tonight with the other captains to the trechandiri (their deposito schooner) and talk with them about going home. We don't want to lose our good catch by getting caught in the late gales." The crew agreed with him. They all had some say because every man got a quarter of the value of his catch. But this year's take weighed in well, and they were satisfied.

Two days later all the small *aktarmades*, like chickens around a mother hen, gathered at night close to the *deposito* and every man went aboard for the farewell feast before beating back north against the autumn winds to the home waters of the far Dodecanese.

VII

A Diver Is Born

THE long voyage home stuck forever in Spiro's mind. After two days of running due north they came to the passage between Kythera and Antikythera which lay off the western cape of Crete and the southernmost point of the Peloponnesus. In the afternoon the wind suddenly switched into the northeast and began to pick up with a low scud racing across the sky. The captains of the *aktarmades* at once sensed trouble ahead and Spiro was ordered about battening down everything movable on deck while a small storm trysail was bent on.

In short order the wind was at gale force and the scum of sea dust whipped across the piling waves. Storms come up quickly in the Aegean. The cool winds from the Bal-

kans in the north meet in turmoil with the warm desert
airs from Egypt. Racing waves pile up steeply and close
together in the passages between the mountainous islands and leave little room for maneuver. But the small
caiques are built for just such conditions and their great
sheer with the high bow and stern plus the flaring sides
let them take the steep choppy seas without shipping too
much water aboard.

But before that night was through Spiro wished he
were on a bigger vessel. The crests of the towering waves
whipped into his face as he crouched behind the cabin
hood of the companionway. Captain Nicholaus and
Costa, who took turns at the tiller, lashed themselves to
the stanchions so as not to be swept overboard. It was
pitch black and no shore beacons were in sight. There
was only the howl of the wind and the sickening rise and
sudden falling away of the stanch little *Basileos*. They
kept her on a starboard tack that would bear her off shore
and eventually the next day, with luck, let them creep in
behind the lee of Milos. It was too late when the storm
struck to run for the shelter of Kythera.

As suddenly as the storm came up, it blew itself out
about dawn. But the sea was still an awesome sight as the
waves raced by the rolling little vessel. Only two others

of the small fleet were in sight. But about breakfast time the waves moderated and they picked up the welcome hull of the *deposito* schooner just to the northward, and by noon the other two *aktarmades* were spotted to the east. As the day wore on the fleet reassembled and the lights of Milos pricked into view on the horizon.

Now all at once Spiro's mind was free of the African reefs and all the life of the past six months. He could think of nothing but Kalymnos and the decisions he would have to make when they came to port and the winter schooling or the job with Apostolis came up. Spiro wasn't much used to making important decisions. So far in his life things had just sort of gone along automatically as he fitted into growing up at Kalymnos. But now the pains of becoming a man were on him. He began to realize that life isn't just a happy accident and that by decisions we make or break our own life. Being a Greek, of course, he was a strong believer in fate. What must be must be, and as to the future, who knows? But the facts were these: Apostolis and his mother would expect one thing of him and the men of the *Basileos* and Costa, he felt now, took it for granted he was one of them. So his feelings were mixed when at last the little fleet picked up the mountains of Kalymnos and on a clear November afternoon swung round the point and headed in past the breakwater toward the blue and white houses that ranged up from the long waterfront.

As they drew near, Spiro could see a crowd of people milling around at the docks and some of the sponge boats which had got home before them blew whistles and waved flags. This was a good homecoming with no tales of death or paralysis to sadden the report of a good season on the banks. Costa, as head *mihanikos*, was up in the rigging, a place reserved for just such an occasion. Spiro could see him straining to pick out the forms of his mother and his girl as the boats shoved proudly in toward the people.

This was a lot different from the send-off last Easter time. Now the boats which had once been so gay with paint were dirty gray hulks. The men were almost black with sun like a lot of bearded pirates. The crowd on the dock was wild with excitement and there was a good deal of *retsina* in the crews who were already on land. No priests this time . . . just families and friends crazy to get together again after six months of anxious separation. Someone turned off the diesel as they slid into dock. People jumped off the boat and on the boat. Costa slid down the rigging and grabbed Krysa in his arms. Spiro ran to his mother who at first hardly recognized him; he had grown and toughened so much by the six months at sea. Then the two brothers and the women made for the house up the hill to get out of the crowd for the family reunion.

That evening Costa and Spiro were wolfing down a

fine homecooked dinner of *marides* and freshly caught *calamarakia* fried in oil, with all the fresh fruit and vegetables their mother could collect at that season. Every now and then groups of men would tramp by the house and yell in at Costa to come down to the *tavernas* and dance. This was the traditional thing at the fleet's return and many of the men made a whole night of it, they were so glad to get free of the dirty cramped quarters of the little *aktarmades* and wash the salt out of their systems with the good home wine.

At last a crowd came along following a man playing the *tsambouna* or small bagpipes. Costa hurriedly wiped his mouth and got up from the table. "That would be Takis and the crew," he said, and made for the door.

One of the outsiders stuck his head in the door and yelled, "Bring the kid along. We want Spiro."

Spiro's mother started to object out of habit but Costa said, "Look, he's one of us. Let him come now and I'll send him home before things get too hot. Promise." So the two ran out the door and joined the march down the hill. The town was certainly hopping as the homecoming celebrations got under way. This was the first time Spiro had ever been allowed to do more than listen to it from a distance.

When they got to the *Taverna* Costa and the others crowded in at the door to watch. The place was full of men Spiro knew, from their own small section of the fleet. They were dancing in circles, in pairs or all alone, doing intricate footwork with sudden high leaps and heel slaps. This would go on for hours, as the crowd took turns. Right now it was fun to see them before the celebration got out of hand.

The tavern owner, a landsman, yelled at Spiro, "No kids in here."

But the men from his ship yelled back, "Cut it out, Chris. He belongs with us. He's staying for a while," and in he came. No one made a fuss. They took him for granted and that was what pleased Spiro.

As always happens when sailors from a long voyage hit home port, some of the men got roaring drunk and the place began to take on a rowdy air. Costa tapped Spiro on the shoulder. "Okay, kid. Beat it now. Ma will be worrying." Spiro didn't mind. He knew he had crossed that invisible and unspoken dividing line that on the Greek islands separates the boys from the men.

The next day Spiro was down with the *Basileos* when they went over to the *deposito* and helped unload the sponges to take to the warehouse for weighing and judging. They would be sold at auction to the different processors except those, like the *Basileos*, which belonged in part to Apostolis who had a stake in the vessel. It was great to watch the brown gunny sacks packed full of African loot go trundling along the waterfront to the long sheds where later they would be cut and culled. Quite a change from the slimy, dark-greenish blobs the *mihanikos* brought up out of the sea.

In the afternoon Spiro strolled along the busy quay and enjoyed letting his less fortunate acquaintances ask him about the season on the African sponge banks. That night his mother asked him if he had seen Mr. Apostolis yet but he told her no, that he was probably too busy buying the sponge harvest. Besides there was plenty of time, he needed rest. He really didn't need rest and his mother knew it and turned away with a sour smile.

A few days later Spiro was hanging around the banking office on the quay where the crews from the various ships were getting paid off with their shares of the voyage. When Costa and the *Basileos* crew were lining up at the door Spiro wandered over by the waterfront. He felt a little left out, for he knew that only the regular crew men were ordinarily cut in on the profits. His small deck-boy wage would be paid by old Nicholaus later.

As he was standing there, Mr. Apostolis came by and called him over. "Well," he said, "the trip did you some good from the looks of it. Did you learn a lot about sponges, Spiro?"

"Yes, sir," said Spiro, "the crew was good to me."

"I've heard so, and that you didn't do so badly yourself." Apostolis grinned at him and put a hand on his shoulder. "We must talk business soon. I'll be free in a day or so."

This was just what Spiro was afraid he would say. He had no ready answer and was about to stammer out something when a man with spectacles came to the door of the bank and yelled at Spiro, "Hey, boy, come over here with the *Basileos* men. We're paying off and I've got a share for you."

Spiro looked dumfounded but Apostolis gave him a friendly push. "It's true. You earned it. Go along with you," and smiled as if he knew more about it than he was saying.

Spiro came in at the tail of the line and up to the window. The clerk was mumbling about all sailors being too dumb to know the value of money and handed him

a fat roll of drachma notes. "Here is your cut. Twelve thousand down to your name. Pretty good for a kid."

Spiro walked home on air, his hand tightly clutching the roll in his pocket. He couldn't wait to get away somewhere in a corner of his house and slowly count it over. This was a fortune to him.

When he got home into the cool dim room of the cottage, Costa and Krysa were there. "Where you been so long?" his mother said.

Costa didn't wait for him to answer, but came over to the table and laid a great wad of money down on it. "We've been paid off. Here is your share, Ma. It was a good year."

Spiro suddenly wanted to be in on it and pulled out his own twelve thousand drachmas, not much compared to Costa's, but plenty, and slapped it down in front of his mother. "And here's my share, too, Ma." He felt like a king. Costa was grinning at him with pride.

The mother picked up all the money in her hands gently and looked at it and tears sprung to her eyes. She kept shaking her head and saying, "Sons, I haven't seen so much money since your father was alive." She counted it over slowly with trembling fingers. "But this is much more than an old woman like me needs."

Just then there was a loud pounding on the door and in came Captain Nicholaus and a young Greek-American whom Spiro knew was a teacher at the diving school. "Hi, Dimitra," the Captain yelled, and came over to the table. "Well, you got two bread-winners now. Things are looking up."

"No, Chris, I can't take it all. The boy will need his when he starts in the factory and has to pay for special schooling. It doesn't belong to me. I'll put it in the bank for him."

"Bank what? Dimitra, you think that boy still belongs landside here in port like some damn cheese-eater? He's one of my crew."

"No. No," she cried, "you can't have him now. Apostolis . . ."

"Now look here, Dimitra, I married your sister didn't I? I knew your old man like a brother, didn't I? I didn't come into a family scared of the sea. I know what you think. Let him be a shop-keeper and safe. Let him get rich. You listen to me. You got plenty. We all got plenty and we live like men. Like men always live from Kalymnos. The fleet will go on, but where are the new captains? This boy can be a captain one day, just like Costa will. I'll take care of this boy."

"That's it, Ma," Costa broke in. "We won't let him get hurt. Besides he's got to go to diving school first anyhow."

The old woman brushed him aside and turned to Captain Nicholaus, "What do you think Apostolis will say to this? He owns half your boat."

"I've seen him," he said. "I've seen him this afternoon and told him all about the trip and what a good seaman we got here. He's not going to kick up. Now remember, Dimitra, when this kid was born and we took him to be christened and the *pappas* held him up by his feet and neck and dunked his little pink bottom in the holy water. Remember, once for the Father, once for the Son and once for the Holy Ghost and then what? . . . that Kalymnos one, once for a good sponge fisherman."

The mother nodded and pursed her lips. The Captain went on, "And what did you say to that then? You smiled and were glad."

"But I had my man then," said Dimitra.

"Yes, Ma," Costa spoke up, "and now you got two men to take care of you."

Spiro had been thinking hard all about this. "Keep my money, Ma, please. It makes me feel good. Then do you know what? Costa and Krysa got enough to get married on right away. How about a big marriage, Ma?"

And Captain Nicholaus couldn't keep quiet either. "Then the family begins again and you got grandchildren for your old age. How long you been telling me you couldn't wait till you had a big family around you again?"

Dimitra smiled a little and looked at Costa and Krysa. The girl said, "I'm for it too. Our men belong at sea. We don't want men that don't go to sea."

Then quickly Costa grabbed hold of the young instructor from the diving school and he introduced him to his mother. They all sat down to the table together.

"Let me tell you something, Mrs. Dimitra," said the teacher. "We are beginning to teach scuba diving without all this helmet and hose business. Maybe your son here will never have to go down in a *mihanikos* outfit."

"Okay, so what?" she answered with a shrug. "He gets bends maybe all the same."

"No, ma'am, not if he's trained to this. The Captain can have two or three men down with plenty of time to decompress and get more sponges than the old way. If the government does something about this it's going to be pretty good for the divers."

"I hope you're right," Dimitra answered him. "I hope you're right. I suppose I've got to let him go with all these men after me, anyhow." She wiped a tear from her nose and turned around to the table and plunked down a bottle of ouzo and set glasses for everybody. She picked up hers and turned to Captain Nicholaus and crossed herself. "*Yasou*, Chris. To the *Basileos* and all her men."

And all her men drank down their *ouzo* and crashed their glasses on the floor. "*Yasou*, Dimitra. *Yasou*, Krysa. *Yasou*, Spiro."

GLOSSARY OF GREEK WORDS USED IN THIS BOOK

(Words italicized in explanations are also in glossary)

aktarma	A special kind of *trechandiri* built for use as a diving boat (pl. aktarmades).
bouzouki	Large musical instrument resembling a mandolin.
caique	Boat of any size, large or small.
calamarakia	Small squid.
deposito	Term used to describe any boat (*caique*) used as a mother ship for sponge-diving boats.
Fernez	Early type diving mask converted from World War I gas mask.
kolaouzeros	The man who handles the *kolaouzos* for the diver (pl. kolaouzeri).
kolaouzos	Diver's lifeline, also used for signaling.
marida	Small fish (pl. marides).
mihanikos	"Machine diver." Term used in Kalymnos for a specialist in diving with the *skaphandro* (pl. mihaniki).

moutsos	Ship's boy.
ouzo	Anise flavored aperitif.
pappas	Priest (pl. pappades).
retsina	Resinated wine.
si-yia	Drinking toast.
skaphandro	Helmet diving suit (pl. skaphandros). Also applied to divers.
sfungaria	Sponges.
taverna	A place where people go to drink wine with appetizing small dishes.
trechandiri	A common type of hull shape in the Greek islands. All trechandiria, whatever their size, are double ended and built to formula: length overall is one-third longer than length of keel, and width is one-third of the length.
trechandira	A large *trechandiri* built for carrying cargo.
tsambouna	Bagpipe.
yasou	Drinking toast — "To your health!"